The Reluctant Biographer

Also published by Slightly Foxed

The Christmas Fox I:
Ghost Writer
by Tim Mackintosh-Smith

The Reluctant Biographer

Jeremy Lewis

Design by 875 Design

First published in 2006 by
Slightly Foxed Limited
67 Dickinson Court
15 Brewhouse Yard
London EC1V 4JX
www.foxedquarterly.com

(10 DIGIT) ISBN 0-9551987-2-0
(13 DIGIT) ISBN 978-0-9551987-2-4

Printed and bound by Smith Settle, Yeadon, West Yorkshire

The Reluctant Biographer

I spent much of my working life as a publisher's editor of the old school, keen on long and bibulous lunches and prone to publish books that got enthusiastic reviews but sold in their hundreds rather than in their tens of thousands; and when, in 1989, I was eventually booted out of Chatto & Windus, I had to bend my mind to other ways of earning a living.

Among those offering advice was a fellow-publisher, a former Olympic fencer who was famously fertile in ideas. For no apparent reason, he had got it into his head that I ought to write biographies. I tried to explain that although I was a passionate devotee of memoirs and autobiographies, I hated reading biographies, thought them inherently second-rate and second-hand, and had no desire to write the wretched things. Carried forward on a tidal wave of eloquence, I went on to say that I regarded biography as the most ephemeral of literary forms, with Boswell and Lytton Strachey the exceptions that proved the rule, and resented the ludicrous claims made on its behalf by eminent modern practitioners; but he would not take 'no' for an answer.

He rang me up one day, sounding more overcharged than ever. He had, he revealed, the perfect subject for me, and would like to unveil it over lunch in a restaurant in St Martin's Lane. After the drinks had been ordered, he put his elbows on the pink tablecloth, gazed deeply into my eyes, and told me what he had in mind. 'Jeremy,' he said, in a tone of grave sincerity, 'you are tailor-made to write a biography of the Duke of Edinburgh, and I could pay you a very large sum indeed to do so.'

Rather ungraciously, I greeted his suggestion with derision. I had, I told him, nothing whatsoever against the Duke – in fact I rather admired him for his tactless remarks – but I had no interest at all in the Royal Family, and could think of nothing I would like to do less. He was quite unfazed by this brutal rejection, but at the pudding stage he suggested, out of the blue, that I should write instead a biography of Cyril Connolly, a literary man remembered, above all, for his greed, his sloth and his complicated love life, and for two marvellous books, *Enemies of Promise* and *The Unquiet Grave*.

It seemed ungrateful to say 'no' twice in the course of a single lunch – and, despite my dislike of biographies, Connolly was an appealing subject. I'm not sure I would have liked him – he would, I felt certain, have gazed anxiously over my shoulder in search of stronger meat – and sometimes, when eventually writing his life, I felt I needed a good bath after too long an immersion in a rarefied, treacherous, self-obsessed world in which everyone was related to and had affairs with everyone else. Still, I found his merciless self-knowledge and his romantic yearnings immensely sympathetic, as well as his refusal to commit himself to any one point of view ('I believe in God the Either, God the Or and God the Holy Both,' he once announced). We agreed that I would do a little background reading, and I headed off to the London Library to see what they had on the shelves.

A few weeks later I had a call from Deborah Rogers, Connolly's literary agent. She told me, in the kindest possible way, that it was a waste of my time to take things any further, since Connolly's widow, Deirdre Levi, was opposed to the whole idea of a biography, and could stymie any attempt by refusing the biographer permission to quote from her late husband's work. I capitulated at once – I couldn't bear the idea of doing battle with an enraged literary widow, a notoriously ferocious breed, and since the only point of a writer is his writing, it seemed idiotic to write a life without being able to quote from the work – and turned my mind to other things.

A couple of years later my phone rang at home, and I found myself talking to an American academic with whom I had been briefly in touch during my abortive explorations into Connolly matters. 'I've just done you a good turn,' he said. An unauthorized biographer had decided to go ahead with a life of Connolly in the face of Mrs Levi's objections. Various friends, including Stephen Spender, had urged her to retaliate by commissioning an authorized biography; she had asked my new friend from Indiana, and he – to my amazement – had recommended me. It seemed too absurd: I wasn't an academic or a professional writer, I had never written a biography before, I knew next to nothing about my subject-to-be, and my literary output consisted of reviews written to pay the bills, introductions to reissues of works by Surtees, Sapper and E.W. Hornung, and a waggish volume of autobiography devoted to my time as an undergraduate at Trinity College, Dublin: why on earth had he chosen me? 'Well,' he said, 'I liked the sound of your voice on the phone.' That seemed as good – or bad – a reason as any, and I gratefully accepted. He urged me to visit Deirdre Levi as soon as possible, and rang off.

By now I was thoroughly in favour of the whole idea, but my heart sank when Mrs Levi – who sounded very likeable, and immediately invited me to lunch near her home in Gloucestershire – asked if I would bring with me a copy of *Playing for Time*, my facetious autobiography. As soon as she said this, I knew the game was up. To my horror, my publishers had given the paperback edition the worst kind of 'comic' cartoon cover, heavily populated by men with bulging eyes and foam-flecked lips and bottles of stout jammed in their pockets. I had no copies left of the more decorous hardback; Mrs Levi would take one look at the cover, realize that I was not a serious candidate for the job, and turn instead to a Fellow of All Souls.

I was working at the time with Alan Ross, the editor of the *London Magazine* and an old friend of both Connolly and his wife, so I took with me a stack of back numbers and dropped my paperback in the middle, like a sliver of supermarket ham in a sandwich, hoping that it would thereby acquire some *gravitas*. The lunch could not have

Alan Ross, the midwife of my new career

been more genial or bibulous. The Levis took me to a quiet country hotel popular with elderly couples: the room was silent save for the click of knives and forks and whispered conversations, but all heads swivelled in our direction as Peter Levi told us, in ringing tones, how Penelope Betjeman had set out for the Himalayas 'with a team of hand-picked lesbians'. Nothing was said about my book until the train for Paddington was about to pull out. I knew that the game was lost as I handed it out of the carriage window with its praetorian guard of *London Magazines*; and as the train trundled back to London I wondered what I could write about instead.

Next day the phone rang, with Deirdre on the other end. 'Peter and I simply *loved* your book, and we couldn't stop *roaring* with laughter,' she said. 'Cyril would have loved it too, still more so since you mention the Cuckmere Valley and Mr Rolfe the fishmonger in Seaford, whom he always visited. Of course you must write his life.' And with that I embarked on my new career. Later I discovered that Deirdre had rung Alan Ross to ask if I'd be the right man for the job: I was a 'good fellow', he said, and that was as far as my scholarly references went.

I had no idea what to do next, but a helpful and experienced biographer friend drew me aside and pointed out that since many of Connolly's surviving friends and contemporaries were, by then, in their eighties and nineties, I should hurry off at once and interview them before it was too late.

Dutiful as ever, I plodded off to see assorted octogenarians, including Peter Quennell, Steven Runciman and the formidable Gladwyn Jebb. The fact that many of them had recently spoken to my rival biographer may have induced a certain lassitude on their part, but even so I soon realized I'd been given dud advice: I knew far too little about Connolly to ask the right questions, while they – very understandably – recycled the same old stories from memoirs of their own. Even the most erudite and well-disposed were prone to amnesia and flights of fancy: early on in the proceedings Isaiah Berlin told me a story which I knew, even then, should have featured Connolly's friend Dick Wyndham chasing Orwell's future wife Sonia Brownell into a duck pond, but which came with the wrong *dramatis personae*.

After a month or so, I decided to call a halt *pro tem.* I would go away and do my homework before undertaking any more interviews. I wouldn't speak to another soul until I had immersed myself in as many published diaries, letters, biographies and memoirs as I could lay my hands on, and once I had familiarized myself with the cast of characters I would trawl through Connolly's voluminous papers in the universities of Tulsa, Oklahoma, and Austin, Texas. If some of the survivors had popped off by the time I got back from the States, that was a risk worth taking:

still more so since I soon realized that although I was perfectly happy to be a voyeur at one remove, riffling greedily through the most intimate letters and diaries, I was far more craven and constrained when faced with flesh and blood, feeling myself to be an uneasy cross between a Peeping Tom and a double-glazing salesman. The fact that Connolly had enjoyed such a complicated love life made the embarrassment factor even greater than it might otherwise have been.

I soon discovered that sitting in libraries is one of the more soothing aspects of the biographer's life. It's very like being back at university, except that one reads to more purpose, and with a greater sense of luxury. Riffling through books and papers, the silence broken only by the dainty coughs of one's fellow-researchers, the turning of pages and the soothing clack of other people's laptops, one inhabits a limbo in which the cares of everyday life have somehow dropped away. But spending long weeks in university libraries in the Mid-West has its drawbacks: at Tulsa the campus was deserted in the evening – the students had all commuted home by car – and once the Special Collections library had closed there was little to do except swim endless lengths in the pool and spin out a lonely meal in the student canteen.

One of the ways in which otherwise obscure American universities have put themselves on the scholarly map is by buying up the papers of eminent writers, and Tulsa had done better than most. Connolly's papers had joined those of Rebecca West, Edmund Wilson, Rupert Hart-Davis and Paul Scott; while I was there a large wooden crate crammed with V. S. Naipaul's paperwork arrived, and I joined the librarians in toasting its safe delivery while a graduate student wielded the crowbar.

Immersing myself in the incestuous, self-regarding world of Eton and Balliol and then emerging into a prairie twilight was a curious sensation, as was coming across letters to Connolly from mutual friends: the Alan Ross file was crammed with his familiar postcards – the message scrawled on a *London Magazine* label pasted over the back of a card from someone else, the writing of which showed through like a palimpsest – and when I tipped it on to my desk they clattered out like so many roofing tiles. Every now and then I contemplated summoning up files from the André Deutsch archive, and rereading memos I had written a quarter of a century before when employed there as a junior editor: but there was never enough time.

I became so addicted to primary sources that I came to believe that one could only trust – or partly trust – letters and diaries written at the time: yet they could be as unreliable as memory itself. Before I imposed my self-denying ordinance, I visited Anthony Powell, who had been at Eton and Balliol with Connolly, and had provided a shrewd if unflattering account of his old acquaintance in his memoirs. I don't think he told me anything I hadn't read in his autobiography, nor – to my disappointment – did he serve up the disgusting-sounding combination of home-made curry washed down with claret and followed by Black Forest gâteau with which, according to proud entries in his *Journals*, he regaled gourmet friends like Roy Jenkins and V. S. Naipaul. Years later, in the last volume of the *Journals*, I found a reference to my visit. After comparing me to a friendly Labrador, he got all the details of my visit wrong. None of it mattered in the least, apart from the Labrador: but so much, I thought, for the reliability of the written word.

Further evidence of the unreliability of both

memory and the written word was provided by another of Connolly's Oxford contemporaries. In one of his volumes of autobiography, the historian A. L. Rowse described how, shortly after publication of *Enemies of Promise* in 1938, Connolly came rushing into his rooms in All Souls and, spotting an annotated copy of his book, eagerly devoured his host's marginalia; after which, wrote Rowse, 'I sat him down to a tutorial on the German mind and philosophy.' None of this quite rang true. Though reconciled to the place in old age, Connolly hated Oxford for much of his life and went there as seldom as possible; the philosopher Stuart Hampshire, who saw a fair amount of him in the late Thirties, was quite sure Connolly never came to All Souls at that time; and Connolly's own papers suggested that the two men were unacquainted. Writing to Lord Astor in 1942, he said that he had never met the waspish academic, but shortly after, following one of his rare visits to

Oxford, he told Billa Harrod that he had 'greatly enjoyed meeting Rowse'. Was Rowse telling a whopper, or were both men equally confused?

Although I knew I would never dare to raise the matter, I decided to pay Rowse a visit while on holiday in Cornwall. Trenarren House was a handsome grey Georgian manor house set in a southwards-facing cleft in the hills; before it, a well-shaved lawn led down to rhododendron bushes, and beyond them shimmered the sea. I was let in by the housekeeper, Phyllis, a talkative Cornishwoman in her eighties, limping on a stick. She explained that her master spent most of his time in bed, seldom venturing downstairs even for meals. After a leisurely tour of the house, she escorted me up a broad flight of stairs and into the great historian's bedroom.

It was a large, light room with tall mullioned windows looking out towards the sea. Rowse lay propped up in bed against a barricade of pillows, and he ordered me to draw up a chair and sit alongside him. His face was the colour of ivory, bisected by a pair of old-fashioned horn-rimmed specs, and topped by a quiff of silver hair. He was wearing mauve and white striped pyjamas, with a loosely knitted shawl draped round his shoulders. He started talking as soon as I came into the room, every now and then laying his hand on my knee or making a camp gesture with his wrist, like a railway signal returning to the horizontal. This latter was often accompanied by laughter, and a curious high-pitched hoot.

'I know all about you, dear,' he said after a while. 'You're a second-rater who read English at Oxford, and thinks he knows all the answers.' 'No, I'm not,' I replied, 'I'm a second-rater who read history at Dublin, and knows next to nothing.' This seemed to please him a great deal: he let out a shriek, murmured something about the superiority of historians to Eng. Lit. academics,

'A terrible old devil': A. L. Rowse
(courtesy of the Estate of A. L. Rowse)

and promptly fell asleep. While he dozed, I got up and paced about the room, examining his books and pictures and gazing out to sea, half-wishing I was in it. When he woke up, we reverted to his favourite subject, the prevalence of second-raters. 'Who is more overlooked by the third-rate Eng. Lit. academics – Cyril or me?' he wondered.

My wife and a friend turned up to collect me, and, the interview over, Phyllis provided another guided tour. 'He's a terrible old devil,' she told us apropos her temperamental master as we poked about the scullery. 'You should hear him when he's angry!'

On the way out, we came across Rowse clinging to the banisters, halfway down the stairs: he was still in his pyjamas, his silver hair shooting from his head like a parakeet's crest, his spectacles flashing fire. 'Who *are* these people?' he demanded. 'Have they come to see you or *me?*' Unawed by his wrath, Phyllis ordered him back to bed, making shooing motions at him with the backs of her hands.

I never saw Rowse again, but until he suffered a stroke from which he never really recovered, we engaged in an affectionate correspondence. For some reason he had decided that I was, if not a first-rater, at least a kindred spirit, suggesting ideas for future books and urging me, without success, 'not to go in for Cyril's habit of self-deprecation – very middle class – which La Rochefoucauld knew was only a way of recommending oneself'. As for the vexed issue of the meeting in All Souls, 'You are quite right, Cyril had only met me and could say tactfully that he didn't know me . . .' It seemed wiser and kinder to let sleeping dogs lie: in one of his letters, Rowse had included a book of his poems, and from them I got a sense of how, behind the boasting and the bombast and the ridicule of second-raters, there lurked a shy, virginal creature who felt himself to be both unloved and unlovable, and who had craved, but never known, physical and emotional affection. 'I have been wondering how you were getting on – slow coach, too meticulous,' he wrote in his last letter to me. I wish he had lived to read my biography, though it's too heavy to read in bed and he would have thought it far too long.

All this lay in the future: back home from my American labours, I was far better equipped to interview survivors: names which meant nothing to me when I started out had become as familiar as those of my own acquaintances, and I knew enough of the details of Connolly's life to ask the right questions, and to know when I was being fobbed off with a self-aggrandizing half-truth.

Among those I would have to beard was Cyril Connolly's second wife, Barbara Skelton, a notorious *femme fatale* to whom the adjective 'pantherine' was usually attached. She had been married to Cyril Connolly, the publisher George Weidenfeld and Derek Jackson, the millionaire Oxford don and amateur jockey; her lovers had included King Farouk (who beat her with his dressing-gown cord), Felix Topolski, Peter Quennell, Alan Ross and Kenneth Tynan. Her alarming reputation seemed to be borne out by her memoirs, comical and bitchy in equal measure, and by her tawny-haired, high-cheeked, almond-eyed good looks, suggesting a ferocious ice maiden painted by Cranach.

She was living in France, so, with Alan Ross's encouragement, I dropped her a line and asked if we could meet. We did so in London, and I was much taken with her silvery laugh, her innate good sense on literary matters, her slim but voluptuous figure – she must have been in her mid-seventies, but her allure was as potent as ever –

The ‘pantherine’ Barbara Skelton

and the snorts of derision with which she dismissed so many of those she had known in that seductive, raffish world where Bohemia and Society intersect. Connolly, as I soon discovered, had been the love of her life, and although she ridiculed his foibles, she always spoke of him with affection and admiration.

Back in France, she urged me to come and stay in her house south of Paris. She told me that I must on no account allow her 'pussers' – a pair of bad-tempered Burmese cats – to escape into the garden. We drank a great deal, and I noticed how, when standing in the kitchen, she endlessly wiped immaculate surfaces with a wad of kitchen paper. She didn't seem particularly interested in discussing her life with Connolly; but then, as if opening a treasure chest, she suddenly showed me a window-seat crammed with plastic shopping-bags, each of them bulging over with his letters, hurled in higgledy-piggledy, with or without envelopes attached. 'I *might* – just might – let you look at these one day,' she said, in her taunting, half-teasing way; and with that she closed the window-seat, and turned to other matters.

Later that summer, she decided to move back to England: she was lonely in France, she hated the 'Frogs', and life might be better on the other side of the Channel. One day she rang and asked if I would do her a great favour: would I help her to pack up, and drive her and the pussers back to London, where she had taken a flat off the King's Road? Happy to escape from my desk, I jumped on a bus and headed towards the Calais ferry.

Barbara was in a filthy mood when I arrived – clad in a dressing-gown, hemmed in by crates, clutching a brimming glass of whisky, emanating ill humour. I soon learned that the only antidote to her sulks was to make her laugh: as it was, she smouldered noisily while I cleared the place and then, awash with whisky, we loaded the back of her Renault Clio with dresses, boots, boxes, the pussers in their cage, books galore, a Toulouse-Lautrec drawing and, teetering uneasily on top of it all, a Sidney Nolan painting of a lugubrious-looking water-fowl picking its way through a swamp. Kitted out with a pair of string driving-gloves, Barbara took the wheel, but after shooting past the Calais exit on the *périphérique* and attempting a U-turn in a motorway maintenance area filled with gravel, she ordered me to take the wheel. As we sped in a northerly direction, she refreshed herself from the whisky bottle and barked out commands to drive 'Faster, faster.'

Back in London, high up in a hideous tower block at the bottom end of Sydney Street, she found herself even lonelier than in France. Over the years she had managed to offend many of her old acquaintances, and those who had not taken umbrage were, more often than not, no longer around to help drain the whisky bottle. My wife

'*Now* what's Cyril saying?':
Cyril Connolly and Barbara Skelton

and I soon discovered we had become extremely fond of Barbara, in the nervous, uneasy way in which one might become fond of some beautiful undomesticated animal that was liable to whip out its claws at any moment. 'Well, *you're* not much of a friend, are you?' she'd say if I failed to ring every other day at least.

She remained as flirtatious as ever, but if I gave her so much as a formal peck on the cheek she went quite rigid, as if she'd been plugged into the mains. One day, greatly daring, I raised the subject of my reading the letters in the plastic bags. She brooded for a while before coming up with a solution satisfactory to us both. She had never been able to read Connolly's handwriting: she would allow me to read his letters on condition that I typed them out at the same time; that way we could both enjoy them. It seemed a dotty idea – there were hundreds of letters, jumbled together and hopelessly out of order, and matters were made worse by Connolly's refusal to date them – but there appeared to be no alternative. Barbara lent me her old portable, stretched herself out on the bed, and, using her dressing-table as a desk, I began to work my way through the mound.

Barbara soon became bored by the proceedings. '*Now* what's Cyril saying?' she would ask; I would read out bits from the letter in question, Barbara would give a shriek of mirth ('So *that's* what he was up to!') and, with luck, place the letter in some kind of context. But it was, I knew, a doomed venture: after a week's typing, endlessly interrupted, I had barely made an impression on the great wodge of sky-blue airmail letters. At this rate, I would spend the next ten years at least working on my biography; some other way round would have to be found.

After Barbara's death I was presented with a complete transcript of those troublesome letters by a mutual friend who knew how much I wanted to read them, could decipher Connolly's spidery scrawl, was a far quicker typist than I could ever be, and – miraculously – managed to put them in some kind of order after much quizzing of postmarks; they were not the most edifying documents, revealing Connolly at his most treacherous and self-pitying, but without them my biography would have been very much the poorer.

That was not the end of the affair. Barbara had also given me various diaries and papers of her own, and these included some unkind remarks about her second husband, George Weidenfeld. Although she had left Connolly for his publisher, with whom she had become briefly infatuated, their marriage had been a brief and wretched affair. I knew, from Alan Ross, how upset

Weidenfeld had been by her bitchy if comical account of their relationship in her memoirs; and now I was not only reopening old wounds, but adding second-hand salt of my own.

After I'd finished my book, I sent Lord Weidenfeld the relevant pages with a note saying how sorry I was to bring all this up once more, and asking if he could bear to check it for inaccuracies. Weeks went by, and I heard nothing; my publisher wanted to get the book into production; I dreaded a writ for libel, or a terrible cry of rage. I got home one evening, and my youngest daughter, Hattie, told me that a foreign-sounding man had rung a couple of times: could I ring him back? Heart pounding, I picked up the phone and rang Weidenfeld at his home on Chelsea Embankment. A purring, slightly inflected voice told me that the chapter I had sent him was most elegantly done, that he was full of admiration; when I apologized for raising old ghosts he

'A worldly Renaissance pontiff': George Weidenfeld

assured me there was no need to worry, that it was all ancient history, but would I mind terribly if he suggested some very small corrections? Of course not, I cried, bending low with gratitude and pleasure.

He hoped I wouldn't mind, but a particular

date was wrong: no problem. I had misquoted from the Latin: I was happy to stand corrected. Was there anything else in need of amendment? Well, he said, it was rather a pity that I'd made mention of – and here he referred to an unkind observation of Barbara's, culled from the papers she'd left me. It wasn't libellous, and I was loath to lose it, so I said nothing, and the conversation moved elsewhere. 'Now,' he suddenly said, 'I'm going to tell you something in the strictest confidence, and you're not to use it in your book. Do you know who told me, when I was in New York, that Barbara had left me and returned to Cyril?' I didn't, and begged him to reveal all about this key moment in Connolly's career. It was the writer Caroline Blackwood, he said: but that was for my ears only. This was, from my point of view, a fact well worth knowing: while married to Barbara, Connolly was always hoping to seduce Caroline Blackwood, earning himself a sharp kick from her first husband Lucian Freud. Since Caroline Blackwood had recently died, it seemed innocuous enough: but although, unlike the waspish aside to which Lord Weidenfeld had objected, it was a small but valuable part of the jigsaw, I'd promised not to use it; and that, it seemed, was that.

After I put the phone down I wrote George Weidenfeld a brief note of thanks; and I begged him to reconsider the matter of Caroline Blackwood, while assuring him that my lips were sealed unless he changed his mind. A day or two later the phone rang, and the great publisher was on the line. He had a proposal to make, and I craned eagerly forward in my chair: if I would remove that waspish observation of Barbara's, he would allow me to include the Blackwood revelation. I was more than happy to accept his terms; yet although I was immensely relieved to be able to go ahead, my overriding feeling was one of liking and admiration for my partner in the deal.

Despite the carpings of envious competitors, I had always thought him the most glamorous and intelligent of publishers, a worldly, empurpled Renaissance pontiff adrift at a Methodist meeting, and now he had joined my pantheon of heroes.

I was even more grateful to Deirdre Levi, to whom I had posted the typescript in a fever of anticipation. She could not have been more complimentary, but she worried that I might have been pulling my punches towards the end. Connolly's relations with women were entertaining but deplorable – he liked to have several on the boil at once, and would bad-mouth them to each other, while declaring undying passion to them all – and towards the end of his life, when he was living in Eastbourne, he had started his last extra-marital affair. I had tiptoed daintily round it for fear of upsetting Deirdre, but she would have none of it. 'I do think you ought to say more about Shelagh,' she said, so in Shelagh went.

Connolly had remained on good terms with Barbara Skelton to the end of his life. One day, when we were eating lunch in her flat, an envelope was pushed under the door. We both assumed it was a circular, but it turned out to be a note from my rival biographer, whose book had now been completed. Shortly afterwards, Barbara got hold of a proof. 'It's awfully good,' she told me: but then she turned against it so violently that she tore the proof in half after scrawling unkind remarks all over it, and hurled it into the dustbin. I rescued it when she wasn't looking, took it home with me, and started reading with a pounding heart.

It was well-written and full of things I'd missed or failed to notice, but the overall tone was hushed and awestruck. In his last year at Oxford, for example, Connolly spent part of his Christmas vacation in Minehead, where 'Sligger' Urquhart, the Dean of Balliol and a kindly bachelor don of the mother-hen variety, had organized a reading party consisting of himself, Maurice Bowra, the waggish and overbearing Dean of Wadham, and a team of hand-picked undergraduates. Bowra had fallen hopelessly in love with one of the group, Piers Synott, a good-looking Anglo-Irishman whom Connolly described as the 'Narcissus of the Balliol baths', and he sought to woo the object of his passion with a medley of music-hall songs; but, after picking his nose throughout the rendition, the ungrateful youth told his admirer that his feet smelt, and the Dean – by now a 'broken man' – had to be taken by Sligger on a long, restorative walk through the surrounding countryside.

The music-hall songs and the nose-picking are details of the kind that should spell magic to the biographer, and I fell upon them eagerly when trawling through Connolly's papers in the library at Tulsa. To my amazement, my rival biographer, who had riffled through the identical papers a year or so earlier, seemed utterly unmoved by their revelations: Connolly, he tells us, 'seems to have been engrossed in Milton, Plato, Yeats and Proust' while in Minehead – and with that the reading party, freighted as it was with comicality and high emotion, was consigned to oblivion.

The relish with which I hovered over the ignoble details of Bowra's courtship almost certainly indicate an incurable frivolity of mind, evidence perhaps of Connolly's claim that 'No two biographies are alike, for in every one enters an element of autobiography which must always be different': but my rival's high-minded refusal to acknowledge nose-picking and the rest also suggests why so many modern biographies seem so dull. Quite apart from his other qualities, good and bad, Connolly was exceptionally funny, both in print and in person, but my rival's biography seemed a joke-free zone. His tone was unvaryingly reverential: so much so that after a while he wearied of referring to his subject by his surname, and called him 'the critic' instead ('That summer, the critic took his holiday in France . . .').

What so many biographers fail to remember is that psychological insights and the accumulation of details must be accompanied by a modicum of artistry; that the biographer, like the novelist, needs to shape his material, to interlace (if possible) the funny and the poignant, the fast-moving and the slow, the quiet and the noisy. All too often biographers are so intent on hurrying their protagonist through his paces that, like a bad host, they quite forget to introduce us to the subsidiary characters, who are bustled on and off stage without a word about their backgrounds, education, looks, proclivities or mode of dress (than which nothing is more touching and revelatory). A sure and familiar sign that the biographer has failed to make the necessary introductions comes towards the end of his labours: eager to strike a valedictory, autumnal note, he tells us that old friends of his subject have died ('That July, Jim learned that his close friend Colin had died of a heart attack') – but since no mention has been made of Colin until now, the emotional impact is not all that it might have been.

Like many other writers – Auden most famously so – my old friend and colleague D. J. Enright abominated literary biographies: what mattered about a writer was his work, not his life, and lives of writers, unless written by the subjects themselves, were intrusive, trivial, irrelevant and somehow immoral. Dennis enjoyed reading my memoirs (or 'me-moirs' as he called them), but although he always asked politely enough how I was getting on with Connolly, he did so between gritted teeth, and I would hurriedly change the subject in favour of cats, a shared enthusiasm, or the bad old days when we had both suffered under the lash at Chatto & Windus.

Since Dennis died at the end of 2002, I have written two more biographies – of Smollett and Penguin's founder Allen Lane – and now I'm working on a group biography of the Greene family. I have loved every minute; and although half of me still shares Dennis's disapproval, the other half has been utterly corrupted. I combine an uneasy sense that we biographers are, by definition, denizens of the literary second division with the hope that the detailed and sympathetic recreation of someone else's life could be worthy to stand alongside the labours of the great novelists: it attempts, after all, the resurrection of the dead, and what could be more miraculous than that?

JEREMY LEWIS spent much of his working life as a publisher, and was a director of Chatto & Windus for ten years. A freelance writer and editor since 1989, he was the Deputy Editor of the *London Magazine* from 1990 to 1994, and has been the Commissioning Editor of the *Oldie* since 1997; he is also the Editor-at-Large of the *Literary Review*. As well as his biographies he has written two volumes of autobiography, *Playing for Time* and *Kindred Spirits*, and is working on a third.